Bernard's Magic

DICK CATE

Illustrations by

SCOULAR ANDERSON

WALKER BOOKS
AND SUBSIDIARIES
LONDON · BOSTON · SYDNEY

To Margaret and Sue
at the Library
for all their help

First published 1997 by Walker Books Ltd
87 Vauxhall Walk, London SE11 5HJ

This edition published 1999

2 4 6 8 10 9 7 5 3 1

Text © 1997 Dick Cate
Illustrations © 1997 Scoular Anderson

The right of Dick Cate to be identified as author of
this work has been asserted by him in accordance with the
Copyright, Designs and Patents Act 1988.

This book has been typeset in Plantin.

Printed in England by Clays Ltd, St Ives plc

British Library Cataloguing in Publication Data
A catalogue record for this book is available
from the British Library.

ISBN 0-7445-7244-4

Bernard discovers that you don't have to be a magician to make magic happen in this entertaining story.

Dick Cate was born in Ferryhill, County Durham. He was a teacher, for many years, at various schools around the country until his retirement in 1982. His first book for children, *On the Run*, was published in 1973. Since then he has written numerous titles, many of which feature the character Billy Robinson. These include *Old Dog, New Tricks* (Winner of the 1979 Other Award), *Ghost Dog* and *Fibs* (shortlisted for the 1991 Guardian Fiction Award). For Walker, he has written *Rodney Penfold, Genius*. *Bernard's Magic* was shortlisted for the Nassen Special Educational Awards Children's Book of the Year. It is the second in a series of three, the others being *Bernard's Prize* and *Bernard's Gang*. Married, with four grown-up children and five grandchildren, Dick Cate lives in Huddersfield.

Books by the same author

Bernard's Prize
Bernard's Gang

For older readers

Rodney Penfold, Genius

Contents

Chapter 1

Bernard was looking down from his bedroom window, feeling sorry for himself because his mum was going out with Mr Rabbet again.

After they'd first left his dad, she used to stay in quite a lot. They used to watch videos together. Sometimes, for a treat, they went to the Taj Mahal. Mr Singh used to save them the table near the carved wooden elephant and light the candles for them. They used to have some good times. But not any more.

Mr Rabbet's BMW was parked across the street, its top shining under the streetlight because Mr Rabbet made a man at his factory clean it every day. Bernard's mum said it could go a hundred and eighty miles an hour. So what? Bernard thought: Mr Rabbet had a baldy head.

"Good night, Bernard!" his mum called from downstairs.

Bernard pretended not to hear.

"Are you asleep, Bernard?"

How could he be asleep when it was Dress Rehearsal tomorrow? And the day after that the real thing!

"We haven't all day," he heard Mr Rabbet say. He'd probably be looking at his watch.

Now Bernard could hear his mother's high heels clattering towards the front door. She was wearing a very short skirt and loads of make-up. She didn't actually look like his mother. To be honest, she didn't look like *anybody's* mother.

"Got to look my best!" she had said when they were waiting for Mr Rabbet to come.

"For Bunny Rabbit!" said Aunty Rita.

And they both laughed. Which Bernard thought was definitely unfair because two weeks ago when Mr Rabbet had first come to their house his mum had told him *never* to call him Mr Rabbit.

"Rabb*et*," she'd said. "Not Rabb*it*. Whatever you do, don't call him Rabbit. Ever."

"Why not?" Bernard had asked.

"Because he might grow big ears," said Aunty Rita.

"His name has an *e* in it," said his mum.

"So has rabbit," Bernard pointed out.

"It hasn't, Bernard," said his mum. "Rabbit is spelt with an *i*."

If this was true it was news to Bernard. All his life he'd spelt rabbit with an *e* and nobody had complained yet. Not even Miss Trim, and last Friday she had shouted at him just because he was still stuck on Brown Level Nine of the Literary Treasure Chest.

Bernard watched his mother cross the road and try the door of Mr Rabbet's car. It was locked, of course. Aunty Rita had said that if it was possible Mr Rabbet would have a lock on his wallet.

His mother looked up at Bernard's window but he had already moved behind the curtain, out of sight. All the same, she waved, as if to show she knew he was watching. Which was fairly typical of his mother.

There was still no sign of Mr Rabbet. Bernard guessed he must have had to go to their downstairs loo. He was a bit like Steven Horsefield at school, who kept having to go

during rehearsals. Squashy Petch had told
Bernard it was because he had something
called stage frights.

His mother was standing by the car now,
talking to a stray cat. She probably hadn't
given a single thought to the Dress Rehearsal.
The whole time Bernard had been downstairs
she hadn't mentioned it once.

Mr Rabbet was crossing the road now,
unlocking his BMW with a flashy gadget that
made *ping* noises. His head was shining
exactly like the top of his car.

He didn't even wave at Bernard before he
got in. This was the third time he'd been out
with Bernard's mum, and Aunty Rita had
hinted it might be the last. Bernard hoped so.

When the powerful engine burst into life
the poor stray cat shot over a wall at a
hundred and eighty miles an hour. As they
drew away Bernard saw his mum waving at
him in a very cheeky manner indeed.

Then they were out of sight and Bernard
told himself, "I'm all alone!"

Chapter 2

Of course, he wasn't quite alone.

Aunty Rita was just downstairs watching one of her videos. Bernard heard a door open with a spooky creak. Followed by a scream.

If he'd gone downstairs and asked to watch, Aunty Rita would have said, Ten minutes, Bernard, but only if you hold my hand!

She was more cuddly than his mum and because of all her previous lives a more interesting person. In one previous life she had been an Egyptian princess and in the one before that a royal cat in China. She could distinctly remember lapping cream from a golden bowl.

She was nuts, of course, but Bernard still liked her.

He wasn't too keen on her videos, though. They tended to be about mummies rising from tombs to seek vengeance, and last week's had been about a foot coming out of a grave.

Bernard had scooted up to bed pretty quickly because it reminded him of the rabbit's foot his grandad had given him. His grandad said it was a rare and precious object and would bring Bernard good luck. Every time he came he asked after it, as if it was a close relation. But personally Bernard wasn't too keen on it because there was what looked suspiciously like blood on one end and he kept having nightmares about the foot escaping from his bedside drawer and chasing him round the room.

Downstairs rumpty-tumpty music started and Bernard snuggled down into bed with the book Louise Bruce had found for him in the school library. It was called *Magic Made Easy* but if this was easy Bernard wouldn't have liked to see it made hard. The first chapter was called Clever Fingers and the first sentence said, "Your clever fingers can achieve amazing feats," which Bernard found confusing. He and Louise had read that much together, but now he was on his own and he felt a bit stuck. Which was a pity because if there was one thing Bernard fancied it was standing on a stage, amazing people. How could you amaze people when you couldn't read the books? As it was, he couldn't even understand the pictures. Under one, for instance, it said, "See that handkerchief?" and Bernard couldn't.

Downstairs the rumpty-tumpty music got even louder and a voice said, "You realize, Professor, that this ghastly creature has come from the dim and distant past to haunt us all? As a medical man, you must agree?"

Bernard pulled the blanket over his ears and tried to think of pleasanter things but thought only about the Dress Rehearsal. Worried about it, really. Because with Bernard, thinking and worrying were more or less the same thing.

"Stop worrying," the new doctor at the hospital kept telling him. The new doctor wore Batman T-shirts and Bernard had to call him Tom. But how could you stop worrying when you were the sort of person who just *did*?

And there were millions of things to worry about.

First, he might catch stage frights, like Stephen Horsefield. Squashy Petch said they just froze you up so you couldn't speak a word.

Or, if he wasn't too scared to speak his words, he would forget them. After all, there were quite a lot to remember. Five. He should have had his brains examined for agreeing to be a Speaking Peasant, but Miss Trim had said "Take a chance, Bernard," and that was exactly what Dr Tom kept saying. He should have listened to the headmaster, Mr Fearby, who'd advised him to be one of the people holding on to the castle wall to stop it falling over.

And if he didn't get stage frights and *did* remember his words there was always his tatie sack. As a peasant he had to wear one. There was no way out because tatie sacks were what peasants wore in the olden days.

Bernard didn't object to wearing a tatie

sack, of course. He wasn't a snob. He was just thinking of his asthma. Which is why his mum had put the sack through the washing-machine three times. So far, it hadn't caused him a sniff of trouble, but if there was one thing Bernard was certain about in this life, it was that you couldn't be certain about anything.

And if, say, he had to use his inhaler in the middle of the play it would absolutely spoil it, because in the olden days they didn't have inhalers, and peasants especially didn't have them.

Of course, as his mother said, none of these things might happen.

And she was quite right. None of them might.

The only trouble was, if none of them happened something else might.

Something a lot worse.

Which was what he was really afraid of.

Chapter 3

Something worse did happen to Bernard at the Dress Rehearsal.

To be exact, *two* somethings.

Firstly, the castle wall fell on his head because one of the people supposed to be holding on to it let go. It's true it was only made of cardboard but as Squashy said afterwards, if it had been made of solid wood he could have been killed.

Secondly, he fell madly in love with Attila the Hun.

Bernard couldn't understand it because for some time now he had been quietly in love with Louise Bruce, who was kind and helpful to people and had eyes like a mouse. In any case, if he'd wanted to fall in love with somebody else the last person he would have chosen was Attila the Hun.

Her real name was Amelia Humm. In the play she was kind Lady Flavia but in real life she was a snobby person on Gold Level Seven.

Normally she never spoke to Bernard. In fact, the last time she'd spoken to him was a fortnight ago when they had both come out to the Literary Treasure Chest at the same time. She had said, "Are you still on Brown Level Nine? I was off that in the baby class!"

But the moment she came on-stage and said, "Have you by chance seen the Royal Messenger?" Bernard fell madly in love and his knees turned to water. It was partly the pong of her mum's scent but mainly the fact that her eyes had gone so blue and misty. It was funny he'd never noticed them before.

Anyhow, Bernard went very red, then very white. Everybody must have seen his knees wobbling. He just managed to gasp his words before falling down the steps at the side of the stage where Mr Fearby was looking up.

"Are you all right, Bernard?" he asked.

Bernard opened his mouth but no sound came out.

"Wouldn't you be better holding up the castle wall? I'm sure we could do with an extra pair of hands after what happened this morning. Shall I get someone from the top class to take your place as Speaking Peasant Number Four?"

Again Bernard just opened his mouth.

"I think you ought to go to the Rest Room, Bernard, don't you?"

There had been a time when Bernard had spent most of his life in the Rest Room. It was nice and clean in there. There was a notice on the door that said GERM FREE AREA. Nobody could get at you and there was a bed. When he had first come to this school Mrs Bell, the school secretary, called it *his* room. She had only to see him coming and she handed him the key. That was before the days of Dr Tom.

Bernard opened his mouth but no sound came out again.

"Slight attack of stage frights," said Squashy Petch when Bernard told him about it at playtime.

"I don't think so," said Bernard.

"How do you mean?"

–21

"I think I've fallen in love."

"Hard cheese. Anybody I know?"

"Attila the Hun."

"Fate worse than death!"

"I think it's her eyes."

"What about them?"

"They were so blue and misty."

"What are you talking about? Attila's eyes aren't blue! Believe me, I know because they give me the screaming abdabs."

"I saw them," said Bernard.

"Maybe you need specs."

"I'm wearing specs," said Bernard.

"Maybe you need better ones. Anyhow, let's not argue about these things," said Squashy, "because I know I'm right. So, what you going to give her?"

"Give her?"

Squashy stared at him for a moment. A look of pity came into his eyes. "I forgot," he said. "You haven't done Orange Level Two."

If only, thought Bernard. "I would have," he said. "I slipped back after my operation."

"I know," said Squashy. "Well, anyway, you have to give her a love token."

"Pardon?"

"It's a token that knights gave maidens in the olden days. When they were in love."

"I see," said Bernard.

"It has to be something precious."

"Money?" Bernard asked anxiously.

He had nine pounds in his money box but he needed that for a new bike. His dad was still holding on to his old one.

"Money's the one thing it can't be."

"Phew!" said Bernard.

"You must have something precious," said Squashy.

"I have!" said Bernard. "My rabbit's foot."

"Pardon?"

"My grandad gave it to me. He says it's rare and precious."

"And you don't mind getting rid of it?"

"It gives me nightmares," said Bernard. "I keep dreaming it's chasing me."

"It sounds the perfect thing," said Squashy.

Chapter 4

At teatime Bernard told his mum and Aunty Rita, who had just popped in, that he had fallen madly in love. His mum said, "Pass the margarine, Bernard, and try to talk sense."

"Aren't you madly in love with Mr Rabbet?" Bernard asked.

"Ha! Ha!" said his mum.

"Mr Rabbet is a thing of the past, Bernard," explained Aunty Rita.

"How do you mean?"

"There's a new kid on the block."

"Who?"

"Tarzan."

"Shush!" said his mum.

"What's Tarzan like?"

"Small," said Aunty Rita, "but perfectly formed."

"*Shush!*" said his mum.

"Has he got any hair?"

"Bags."

"So Mr Rabbet won't be coming again?"

"We shall all miss him dreadfully," said Aunty Rita.

"Money is not the only thing in life," said his mum.

"By the way," said Bernard, "I forgot to tell you. I nearly died this morning – the castle wall fell on my head."

"Surprises are good for you," his mum said.

Bernard could hardly believe his ears.

"How do you mean?"

"They keep you on your toes."

"You mean, castles falling on your head keep you on your toes?"

"Yes," she said. "There's even a song about it. Remember that cowboy film we once watched together?" She sang, "Castles keep falling on my head," then added, "*Butch Cassidy and the Sundance Kid* it was called."

When Aunty Rita popped out to do some shopping Bernard went up to his bedroom to mope because it always worried his mum when he moped. And when he got in his bedroom he stayed dead quiet so she would think he was doing nothing, which always worried her more.

"What are you doing, Bernard?" she called after a bit.

"Nothing," he called back.

"Can't you find something?"

"Like what?"

"Like reading your magic book?"

"Don't fancy it," he said.

In fact, he was already having another go at it because Dr Tom was always saying, "If at first you don't succeed, Bernard, give it another bash." This time Dr Tom seemed to be right because the second chapter was called Where's That Coin? and Bernard romped straight through the first sentence. It said, "This is a trick any fool can do," which he found quite encouraging.

As far as he could make out, you were supposed to insert a pound coin between the first and second fingers of your right hand, but Bernard didn't want to use one of the pound coins in his money box in case he lost it, so he used a ten-p instead. You were supposed to cover the coin with a hanky and he managed that easily.

It was after that when things got tricky. First of all, there were a couple of words that Bernard couldn't quite make out and then three he hadn't a clue about.

As far as he understood, you were supposed to wiggle the hanky, and the coin magically disappeared. But every time Bernard wiggled the hanky the coin magically stayed where it was.

After he had tried it six times he was surprised to hear Mr Rabbet come in, and when he heard him sobbing he supposed it was because he was now a thing of the past.

"Have a cup of coffee, Harry," his mum said downstairs. "That'll make you feel better."

Mr Rabbet sobbed louder.

Bernard tried wiggling his hanky again but when it didn't work again he decided it might be more interesting to watch Mr Rabbet crying.

He took his coin and hanky and book with him so he could practise his trick while he pretended not to be listening, but halfway down the stairs had a brilliant idea and put the coin in his pocket.

Mr Rabbet was sitting by their kitchen table staring at a half-empty milk bottle. The kitchen light reflected from his bald head.

"Hello, Mr Rabbet," Bernard said cheerily. "I'm doing tricks."

Mr Rabbet continued to study the milk bottle.

"Bernard is practising to become a magician, Harry," said his mum.

"How very interesting."

"All I need is a pound coin, Mr Rabbet," said Bernard.

"Bernard!" said his mum.

"Money?" said Mr Rabbet, tearing his eyes from the milk bottle.

"Just one pound," Bernard said reassuringly.

"What have I always told you, Bernard!"

said his mum.

"Just a lend," said Bernard.

"Borrow!" said his mum. "Borrow!"

At first Bernard thought she'd said *burrow*, which wouldn't have been surprising because Mr Rabbet looked as if he'd have liked to dive down a burrow as he slowly pulled out his purse. He also took out a big spotty hanky and for a moment Bernard thought he was going to do the trick himself but instead he just blew his nose. Then after calming his nerves he handed the coin over.

"I've told you never to ask Harry for money!" said his mum.

"It's all right," said Mr Rabbet trying to smile. "I'm sure he can't lose it. Can he?"

Chapter 5

As Bernard sat on their flobby old sofa Mr Rabbet suddenly cried out, "But why does it have to end like this!"

"Don't forget your coffee," Bernard's mum told him.

Bernard carefully inserted Mr Rabbet's pound coin between his first and second fingers.

"Why! Oh, why! I just don't understand!"

"Biscuit?" suggested his mum.

Bernard covered his right hand with the hanky.

"I don't mind a chocolate one," sobbed Mr Rabbet.

Bernard wiggled the hanky and pulled it away – the coin wasn't there.

Stay cool, he told himself.

To be honest, he didn't know whether to be happy or sad. He couldn't help smiling but at the same time he was worried.

It was a great thing to make a pound coin magically disappear, of course. On the other hand, if he didn't make it magically reappear pretty soon his mum would make him pay it back out of his money box.

First, he looked at the back of his right hand to see if it had somehow got stuck there. It hadn't. Neither was it hiding up his sleeve. He remembered putting his ten-p in his pocket as he came downstairs and wondered if he had done the same with Mr Rabbet's pound without thinking? But he hadn't. The ten-p was still in his pocket. The pound wasn't.

As calmly as he could, he stood up and began shoving his hands down the sides of the flobby sofa.

"What are you doing, Bernard?" asked his mum.

"Nothing."

Bernard flung all the sofa cushions on to the floor. His arms were up to the elbows down the sides of the sofa.

"I'm waiting to see that pound coin!" said his mum.

"I've made it vanish!"

"You'd better not have!"

Just then Aunty Rita came in. "Spring cleaning, Bernard?" she asked when she saw him throwing sofa cushions up in the air.

"I've just made a pound coin vanish, Aunty Rita!" Bernard said.

"He means he's just lost it," said his mum. "It's one of Harry's. He's only had it five minutes and he's lost it already!"

"I haven't lost it," said Bernard. "I've made it vanish!"

"Pound coins do not vanish," said his mum.

"This one did!" said Bernard.

"Don't answer back!" said his mum.

A great shuddering sob escaped Mr Rabbet.

"Tell me exactly what you were doing, Bernard," said Aunty Rita.

"First, I inserted the coin between my first and second—"

"What have I done to deserve this!" cried Mr Rabbet and he banged the table and his coffee spilled over. If Bernard had done that his mum would have gone crazy. The tears were streaming down Mr Rabbet's cheeks and Bernard's mum tore off a great length of kitchen roll and handed it to him. "Why are you doing this to me?" asked Mr Rabbet, shooting to his feet.

"Sit, Harry!" shouted Bernard's mum.

"Calm!" shouted Aunty Rita.

"*Why?*" shouted Mr Rabbet.

Bernard's mum forced him back into his chair.

"There!" she said. "There!"

Bernard just wished she'd say something like that to him sometimes.

Sobs still escaped Mr Rabbet but by now they were little ones.

Bernard was still on his knees searching for the coin. Although he couldn't find it, he eventually found himself smiling.

Mr Rabbet wasn't smiling, though. But at least he was returning to normal. After two shudders and a sob he asked anxiously,

"Found that coin yet, Bernard?"

"Not yet," Bernard said.

He tried to sound sad but inside him there was a nice feeling. It was the feeling you get when you do something right, Bernard didn't often get that feeling so when it came it was especially nice. The last time he'd done something right was when he passed the test card to start Orange Level Two (before the operation made him slip back).

"You'd better find it, Bernard!" said his mother.

"Don't worry," said Mr Rabbet, trying to smile. "It must be there, somewhere. The lad can't have lost a pound coin. Impossible. In any case, it's nothing to worry about, is it? I'm sure—"

Aunty Rita suddenly dived into her voluminous shoulder bag. She took out a pound coin from her purse and thrust it under Mr Rabbet's nose.

"What's this?" he asked.

"It's a pound coin, Harry!"

"I know it is, Rita. I'm not daft. I mean—"

"Take it!" she shouted.

"I don't want your pound coin, Rita."

"You do, Harry! Take it, and stop blubbing!"

"This is totally and absolutely unnecessary," he said.

"Take it!"

"I don't want to take one of your pound coins, Rita," he said. "I can't possibly."

But he took it all the same. And put it straight in his pocket.

Which shows he *must* have been back to normal.

Chapter 6

Next morning in the playground, when Bernard showed Squashy his rabbit's foot, Squashy said, "That's supposed to be a love token?"

"What's the matter with it?"

"To me it looks like something from a horror movie."

"It's my rabbit's foot."

"I know what it is, Bernard. You told me yesterday. I'm just trying to be honest. I mean, what's that horrible black stain on it?"

"Paint."

"Paint? Rabbits don't have paint on their feet, Bernard. You know what it looks like to me? Blood. Probably the rabbit's own."

Bernard tried to look amazed.

"It can't be blood," he said, shaking his head.

"I'll be honest with you, Bernard. I've never seen anything less like a love token in all my life."

"What do you mean?"

"It's hard to explain if you haven't done

Orange Level Two."

"It's the most precious object I've got," said Bernard, "apart from my old bike. And my dad's still holding on to that."

"You seriously want me to give that – that *thing* – to Attila the Hun?"

"Yes. And I want you to tell her I'm crazy about her."

"She'll kill me."

"Please, Squashy."

"I just can't do it, man. I'm only human."

"I'll give you a packet of Polos."

"OK."

Bernard hid behind a wall when Squashy called her over.

"What now, Flobface?" she asked.

At least she sounded in a good temper.

"Bernard says he fancies you."

"Tell Bernard from me I think he's a truly revolting specimen. And for your information, he's still stuck on Brown Level Nine," she said.

"I know," said Squashy.

"He'll never get off it."

"I know," said Squashy. "But he wants you to have this."

Bernard heard her scream. "What *is* that thing?"

"What does it look like? It's a rabbit's foot."

"It's a *dead* rabbit's foot!" she said.

"You don't expect it to be alive, do you?" asked Squashy.

"Don't be funny with me, Flobface! You can see where it's been cut off. It's got *blood* on it!"

"Where?"

"There."

"That's not blood. That's black paint."

"You must be out of your tiny mind!"

"Anyhow, he wants you to have it," said Squashy.

"I wouldn't *touch* that thing!"

"It's a love token."

"If you think that's a love token you mustn't have a single clue."

"Here," he heard Squashy say. "Take it!"

He must have pushed it towards her because she screamed again.

"Do that once more and I'll tell the headmaster!"

A moment later, Squashy joined Bernard behind the wall.

"I don't honestly think she fancies you, Bernard," he said. He handed back the rabbit's foot and held out his hand for the Polos.

Bernard handed them over.

"And if I were you, I'd wrap something round that thing."

"What for?"

"You could catch something."

"Like what?" asked Bernard.

"Like death," said Squashy. "There could be germs still pouring out of it. Use paper towels from the bogs. Tons of them. And another thing. She hasn't got blue eyes."

"She has!" said Bernard.

Squashy shook his head.

"Somebody told me last night," he said. "In the Dress Rehearsal she was wearing her mother's contract lenses."

"Contract lenses?"

"Things you shove in your eyes," explained Squashy. "Only Mr Fearby doesn't want her to wear them any more, in case she goes blind."

Bernard wasn't surprised.

Chapter 7

The paper towel in the bogs was thick, strong stuff, just right for keeping germs in, and Bernard was wrapping six sheets of it round his grandad's rabbit's foot when Stephen Horsefield came out of one of the cubicles, looking pale.

"You OK?" asked Bernard, trying to be nice.

"What did you say?" asked Stephen.

"Just wondered if you were worried."

"Worried? What about?"

"About today."

"What about today?"

"It's the play. I just wondered if you were worried about it."

"Who says I'm worried about it?"

"Nobody." Bernard just managed to squeeze out the word. His throat had gone dry. He wondered if this time he really had caught stage frights. (Or could you only catch stage frights on a stage?)

Stephen came over and glared down at him.

"I'm not scared of anything! Have you got that?"

Bernard nodded his head.

He couldn't even squeeze out a yes by now.

"So don't talk to me about being scared," continued Stephen. "You're the only one who's scared of anything round here!"

All of which was perfectly true, of course. Even if he had been able to speak, Bernard wouldn't have denied it.

He felt so shaken and stirred after Stephen had gone that he stood there for ages hearing the swing-door go *whuppety* and when he caught a glimpse of himself in a mirror he looked so white it made him feel even worse. He leaned on one of the wash-basins for support. He felt he might be sick so he reached for his pills and took one.

It was just bad luck that as he came out of the bogs Mr Fearby was galloping down the corridor.

"You look absolutely ghastly, Bernard," he said. "Absolutely! Fit only for the Rest Room.

But it's too late now, of course! I warned you, didn't I?"

Before Bernard could reply he had galloped even further away.

"Anyhow," he called over his shoulder, "I shall be sitting in the front row watching every minute with the chairperson of the governors! You realize, Bernard, that if anything goes wrong it will be an absolute catastrophe!"

Chapter 8

As soon as Attila the Hun came on, Bernard realized he wasn't in love with her any more.

Squashy had been quite right. Her eyes were not blue. They were some other colour. Without her mother's contract lenses she meant nothing at all to him. She was, in fact, a thing of the past.

Everything went fine at first. The castle wall didn't fall down and the peasants who mowed the grass did a very good job.

Everything was fine until Attila said, "Have you by chance seen the Royal Messenger?"

That was the moment in the play when Bernard was supposed to look towards the school piano and see Stephen Horsefield and say, "Hither comes he, Lady Flavia."

There was only one slight snag – Stephen Horsefield wasn't there.

The piano was there. And, in a way, this ought to have been a bit of a comfort but somehow it wasn't. At first Bernard thought he was in the middle of one of his own nightmares. But he wasn't. Stephen

Horsefield definitely wasn't there.

Bernard didn't know what to do. He felt an attack of stage frights creeping up. Then he realized that Stephen had probably nipped to the bogs and would be back soon. He'd just have to delay things a bit.

He looked at Attila and said calmly, "He cometh not yet!"

And he gave her a meaningful wink.

At least, he hoped it was a meaningful wink. But it didn't seem to mean a thing to Attila, who leaned forward and whispered, "You're supposed to say, *Hither comes he!*"

"Fear not!" Bernard told her. "I bring thee glad tidings." It was a line he remembered from some other play.

Attila's mouth fell open.

She looked straight past him at Miss Trim, crouching behind a curtain looking worried.

Louise Bruce, beside her, didn't look worried at all. She was smiling at Bernard. Obviously she had every confidence in him. She even seemed to be urging him on because she was nodding.

Bernard looked back towards the piano in the hope that Stephen had at last turned up. But he hadn't.

Until he did – with the royal letter – Lady Flavia would not be able to return to the castle and unless Lady Flavia returned to the castle they would all be stuck and the play would grind to a halt. Bernard had to do something, and quick. But what? Every eye in the audience was on him, waiting. But what did they expect him to do? Produce the letter out of thin air? That would be magic. He couldn't possibly do that, could he?

Of course he could! It would take some doing. It wouldn't be easy. He would have to use very clever fingers indeed.

He hauled up his potato sack and dug his hand into his trouser pocket. He withdrew his six sheets of paper towel and let them slowly unroll. The way he did it made them look exactly like the sort of royal letter they had in the olden days. At the same time he used his clever fingers to completely conceal the rabbit's foot from Attila's view. One slip, he knew, and she would scream the place down.

"What on earth are you up to?" Lady Flavia asked suspiciously.

"Worry ye not," Bernard told her. "Your father asked me to give you this." He thrust the sheets of paper towel at her. " 'Tis the letter," he explained.

At last she was beginning to get the message. Light was beginning to dawn. As she reached out and took the paper towel Bernard cleverly flicked the rabbit's foot through the armhole of his tatie sack so that it slithered down into his right wellington boot. It was an amazing feat.

"I must return to the palace at once," he whispered to her.

She glanced up at him. At first he thought she wasn't going to take his advice but then she repeated after him in a humble voice: "I must return to the palace at once." Then she exited stage left and the play was saved.

Chapter 9

Not that everybody appreciated it.

As soon as the play ended, Mr Fearby rushed up to Bernard and said, "What on earth did you think you were playing at?"

Naturally, Bernard was shocked. He had been expecting congratulations. Mr Fearby's eyes were sticking out like ping-pong balls.

"I'm sure Bernard did what he thought was best at the time," said Miss Trim, appearing from behind the curtain.

"I'm sure he did! I'm sure he did!"

"I thought it was positively amazing, the way he produced that letter from apparently nowhere."

"Letter? I take it you mean that scruffy bit of paper towel? You realize the chairperson of the governors was present?"

"I do," said Miss Trim. "I also realize that by producing 'that scruffy bit of paper towel' as you call it, Bernard saved the play. I suspect we would have waited a long time for Stephen Horsefield to put in an appearance. Where is he now, by the way?"

"I have not a single clue!" said Mr Fearby. "And while I remember, Bernard, I understand that in the playground this morning Amelia was threatened by some horrible object belonging to you."

"You mean my rabbit's foot, sir?"

"Rabbit's what?"

"Foot, sir."

"Hand it over!"

Bernard bent down and after inserting his rabbit's foot between the third and fourth fingers of his right hand pulled it out of his right wellington boot.

Mr Fearby hesitated for a moment before taking it.

"This – this – object – is confiscated until further notice!" he said as he stamped off. The rabbit's foot didn't seem to bring him much luck either because he fell down the steps as he left the stage and limped across the hall in the direction of the Rest Room.

"Well done, Bernard," said Miss Trim. "Under the circumstances, I think you did what was best. I thought it was – well – amazing. And I'm sorry about shouting at you last Friday. We'll have another go at Brown Level Nine tomorrow, shall we?"

"Yes, Miss."

And as she wandered off, Louise Bruce appeared from behind her.

"I just want to say I thought you were wonderful," she said.

"I know," said Bernard.

"I thought you were magic."

It was funny she should use that word.

Chapter 10

Bernard was looking down from his bedroom window at Tarzan's car parked under the streetlight. Tarzan and his mum were going to the Taj Mahal.

His dad would have called Tarzan's car a rust-bucket if he'd seen it. Not that he had a dad any more. Not really.

In any case, he liked Tarzan. While Tarzan had been waiting for his mum to get ready he had sat on the busted sofa with Bernard and read a whole chapter from *Magic Made Easy*. He'd even shown Bernard the handkerchief in the picture where it said, "See that handkerchief?" It had been there all the time, half hidden up somebody's sleeve. Amazing.

Now his mum and Tarzan were crossing the road together. Bernard was pleased to see that the top of Tarzan's napper was entirely covered with hair. Unless it was a wig. You could never tell with adults. Tonight, for instance, just before Tarzan arrived, his mum had decided to be twenty-nine again.

"You were thirty-five last birthday,"

Bernard reminded her.

"I know, Bernard. But from tonight I'm twenty-nine."

"I don't get it."

"It's called second childhood, Bernard," said Aunty Rita.

"I've decided to put back the clocks," said his mum.

"How exactly old is this Tarzan?"

His mother looked at him – and it was clear to Bernard that until that moment she hadn't realized how smart he really was.

"Twelve," said Aunty Rita.

"You mean he's still at school?" said Bernard.

"He ought to be," said Aunty Rita, "if he goes out with someone as ancient as your mother."

"Thank you for that kind support!" said his mum.

Just before she climbed into the rust-bucket she looked up at Bernard and smiled. Even Bernard had to admit she didn't look thirty-five. She looked younger tonight than he could ever remember.

She waved and Tarzan waved as well. He waved as if he meant it. Not like Mr Rabbet used to.

And Bernard waved back.

Tarzan had said that the next time they went to the Taj Mahal Bernard should come with them. Just the three of them. For a treat.

There were a lot of very loud noises when Tarzan tried to start his engine but the car didn't actually move. Even from here Bernard could hear his mother giggling. In some ways she was like a child.

Then, just when Bernard thought they were never going to go, the engine burst into sort-of-life and they stuttered down the street.

When they vanished round the corner Bernard thought, I'm all alone!

Chapter 11

But of course he wasn't. Aunty Rita was just downstairs watching another of her videos.

She had been quite right about Tarzan, Bernard thought. He was small but perfectly formed – the sort of Tarzan you would expect to find in a small but perfectly formed jungle.

And Bernard couldn't understand at all how he'd done the trick. He'd done it when Bernard's mum had come downstairs and blabbed about Bernard losing the pound coin. Just as she said, "We looked everywhere," Tarzan had leaned forward and pulled a coin from Bernard's ear: "This the one?"

It couldn't have been, could it? Not the same coin. If it had been stuck in his ear that long he would have noticed. Wouldn't he?

But if it was just a trick, where had Tarzan got the coin from? From his own pocket? But how had he managed to do that? Bernard didn't want to think about it too much. He preferred to think it was magic.

He wondered if they were in the Taj Mahal by now. He imagined them sitting at the little table by the carved wooden elephant. Mr Singh had lit the candles for them and Bernard could see the golden light on his mum's face as she told big lies about her age.

He hoped they would have a good time. He felt they would.

It was funny to think that instead of being a flop in the play, he'd saved it. As long as he lived, he'd never forget the moment when he realized the whole audience was watching him, wanting him to do something. And he had.

And Miss Trim had been quite right about Stephen Horsefield. They would have waited a long time for him to deliver the letter. After tea Squashy had told Bernard that Stephen had run all the way home and locked himself in their upstairs bog and wouldn't come out till *Neighbours* started. Which showed how serious it really was.

Altogether, Bernard felt, it had been a good day. He'd fallen out of love with Attila the Hun, which was a relief. And he was glad he had fallen back in love with Louise Bruce.

And he'd got rid of his grandad's rabbit's foot at last. With a bit of luck he would never get it back again. And he was a pound coin better off because when Tarzan had found the one in his ear he had offered it back to Aunty Rita but she had refused to take it. She said she had plenty of money. Which was nice.

Downstairs on Aunty Rita's video a spooky door opened and a woman screamed but Bernard wasn't worried. When a voice said, "You realize, Inspector, that this ghastly creature is now stalking the marshes, looking for us?" Bernard couldn't really care less.

He didn't feel scared any more. He felt a new chapter had opened in his life. And he had a feeling that tomorrow he would be off Brown Level Nine for ever. Which would be really something.

Downstairs, a man said, "We are none of us safe in our beds, Amanda."

But Bernard didn't care.

He felt safe in *his* bed. He felt amazing.

He felt magic.